216 NE Knott St, Portland, OR
503-988-5021

Philipp Winterberg   Nadja Wichmann

Am I small?

**AVAILABLE FOR EVERY COUNTRY ON EARTH
IN AT LEAST ONE OFFICIAL LANGUAGE**

English (English)

Translation (English): Philipp Winterberg

Text/Publisher: Philipp Winterberg, Münster · Info: www.philippwinterberg.com · Illustrations: Nadja Wichmann
Fonts: Patua One, Noto Sans etc. · Copyright © 2016 Philipp Winterberg · All rights reserved. No part of this book may be
reproduced, stored in a retrieval system, or transmitted by any means without the written permission of the author.

This is Tamia.

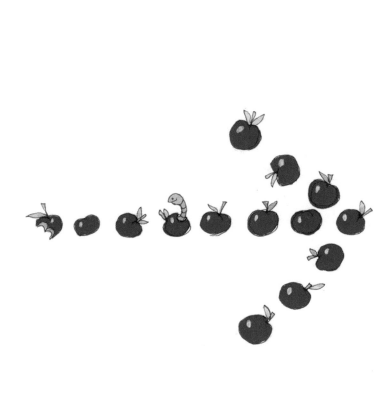

Right!
Exactly!

Tamia is still very small.

Me?
Small?

Am I small?

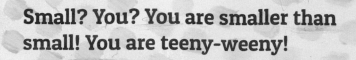

Small? You? You are smaller than small! You are teeny-weeny!

Teeny-weeny? You?
You are mini!

Am I teeny-weeny?

Mini? You?
You are tiny!

Am I mini?

Am I tiny?

**Tiny? You?
You are microscopic!**

Am I microscopic?

Microscopic? You?
You are big!

Am I big?

Big? You?
You are large!

Am I large?

**Large? You?
You are huge!**

Am I huge?

Huge? You?
You are gigantic!

Wait a minute...
I've got it!
I'm everything...

...and if I'm everything, I'm also: just right!

More Books by Philipp Winterberg

  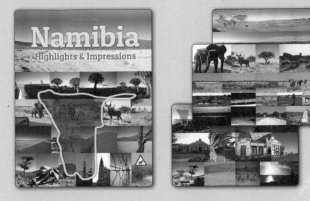

MORE » www.philippwinterberg.com

CPSIA information can be obtained
at www.ICGtesting.com
Printed in the USA
LVHW06n0057210318
570603LV00003B/22/P